AESOP'S FABLES

The Fox and the Grapes

D0572784

Adapted by Ronne Randall
Illustrated by Louise Gardner

p

One warm summer's day, Red Fox went out into the forest. He was a handsome young fox and very proud of his thick red coat and fine bushy tail.

He was strolling along the forest path, looking for something to do, when he spotted some fluffy little bunnies just coming out of their burrow.

"Perfect for chasing!" thought Red Fox and scampered after them. But they were too fast for him.

"You can't catch us!" they giggled, as they darted away.

"Who cares about a bunch of silly bunnies?" thought Red Fox. "Rabbits are never any fun. I'll look for something else to chase!"

So, Red Fox plodded slowly along the path, until he spotted two bushy-tailed squirrels, busily burying acorns.

But the squirrels heard Red Fox and scampered quickly away before he could get near them!

"You can't catch us!" they chuckled,
as they pelted him with acorns.

"Oh, who cares about a couple of silly squirrels?" thought Red Fox. "If I had caught them, they would have given me nothing but trouble anyway. I'll find something else to do!"

So, Red Fox continued until he came to the edge of the forest.

"I've never been out in the big, wide world," he thought. "I'll bet I can have lots of fun out there!"

Red Fox strolled across a field until he came to a wide, dusty road. "I wonder where this leads," he thought, so he decided to follow it.

As he walked, Red Fox looked all around him. He saw some fuzzy field mice, scurrying through the tall grass…

…and then suddenly, he heard a loud rumbling and clattering that made the ground shake and his toes tingle.

Red Fox was frightened!

He'd never heard such a terrible noise before and he wondered if the earth was going to swallow him up!

But it was only a farmer's cart.

As soon as it passed, everything was quiet again and Red Fox went on his way.

As Red Fox trudged along, the blazing sun beat down on his back.

He soon grew hot and thirsty and, before long, his empty tummy began to rumble and grumble. "I haven't eaten anything for hours," moaned Red Fox. "And the hot sun and dusty road have made my mouth *so* dry...

"…I wish I could find something sweet and juicy to eat."

Suddenly, Red Fox smelled something wonderful. It was sweet and tempting and it made his mouth water.

He followed his nose across the road, right to where the smell was coming from.

Red Fox found himself in the garden of a tiny house.

At the side of the house was a leafy grape vine, with big bunches of ripe, purple grapes hanging down. Red Fox couldn't believe his luck!

"Yum, yum!" said Red Fox, licking his lips.

"Those grapes look *so* sweet and juicy. They are just what I need to quench my thirst and fill my empty tummy!"

"I'll have to really stretch myself to reach those grapes," said Red Fox, "but I'm *sure* I can do it!"

He stood under the grape vine and reached up as far as he could.

He stretched... and stretched... and s-t-r-e-t-c-h-e-d.

But even standing on the very tip-toes of his hind legs, Red Fox couldn't reach the grapes.

"Stretching won't work," grumbled Red Fox. "I know, I'll just have to jump!"

So, he jumped h-i-g-h into the air.
But he *still* couldn't reach the grapes.

Once again, Red Fox looked up at the
grapes, which hung just out of his reach.

They looked more delicious than ever
and Red Fox *knew* he had to
have some, no matter what
it took.

"I must jump
higher this time,"
he thought.

So, he leapt up into the air,
just as high as he could.
But he **still** couldn't reach
those plump, juicy grapes!

Red Fox was tired with thirst and hunger, but he couldn't give up now. The grapes looked sweeter and juicier than ever.

"I'll try one more time," he said. "And this time, I'm *sure* to reach them!"

Red Fox reared back on his hind legs and sprang high into the air.

But *still* he could not reach those gorgeous grapes.

Exhausted and miserable, Red Fox gave up at last. With his head hanging down, he slowly slunk off down the hot, dusty road.

"Oh, who wants a bunch of silly grapes?" he said. "They were probably sour, anyway!"

And, hungrier and thirstier than ever, he trudged wearily back to the forest.